For Wendelin and Mark, who add
leaf after leaf to my thankful tree
–N.S.

For Jacob and Sammy
–S.G.

ISBN 978-0-06-295676-7

The artist used a mix of handmade props and photography to create the illustrations for this book.
Typography by Dana Fritts
20 21 22 23 24 RTLO 10 9 8 7 6 5 4 3 2 1 ❖ First Edition

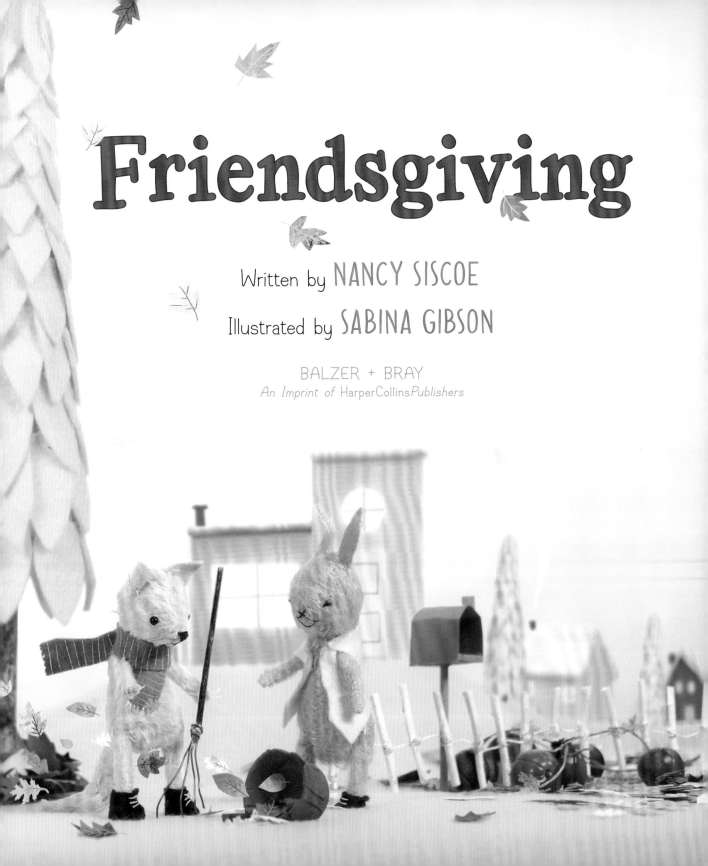

Friendsgiving

Written by NANCY SISCOE

Illustrated by SABINA GIBSON

BALZER + BRAY
An Imprint of HarperCollins Publishers

The air was so crisp, and the sky was so blue, that Ginger, Berry, and Willow knew just what they should do.

"Let's go for a bike ride!"

"How 'bout
Lookout Hill?"

"Ooh! Wonderful!"

They sped along roads lined
with orange, yellow, and red.

Then they pedaled uphill
to the very top,

and stopped, and flopped.

"It was worth the climb for
this view of the town."

"Phew!!"

"It was worth the climb so
we can zoom back down!"

A day spent riding will make you hungry,
so they all agreed the farmers' market
was the place to be.

"Cinnamon
bread for me."

"Cheese, please!"

A great day in fall gets even greater
when old friends meet new friends
and make plans for later.

"Everyone, meet Rowan—
we started a donut stand!"

"Honey! Hello!"

"Sweet!"

"We should
get together!"

Willow was mulling some cider,
and Berry was lighting a fire,
when Honey and Rowan blew in
on a cold gust of wind.

"Come in!"

"We brought some
leaves with us."

"We'll add them to our collection."

"Collection?"

The friends had started a thankful tree.

"When you think of something you're thankful for, you write it on a leaf and add it to the tree."

At the orchard, they picked Empires,
Cortlands, Gravensteins. . . .
Willow had never seen so many varieties of apples!

"One bag or two?"

"Or three or four!"

"Oh my gosh,
a McIntosh!"

"Any more you'd
like to try?"

"Let's go home
and make a pie!"

All those apples to peel and core—
dice one up, then slice some more.

Willow was good at rolling and crimping.
Rowan could handle the cutting and sprinkling.

"Apple pie or apple crisp?"

"Is this a taste test?"

"Both are best!"

The next day was spent making
great piles of leaves that inspired leaping.

They jumped and laughed even though they knew that now they had more raking to do.

"Woo-hoo!"

"Let's do it again!"

Before the first frost, Berry brought in the last harvest
and put their garden to bed for the winter ahead.

Then one more thing—a thought for spring.
He planted bulbs for crocuses and daffodils
so flowers would follow winter's chills.

crocus

daffod

Berry's harvest was so big, it was clear to see they had to share this bounty.

"Let's have a party!"

They made invitations and decorations—
oh-so-many preparations for an autumn celebration!

"More important—
what should we have
for dessert?"

"I would try a
pumpkin pie. . . ."

"What should we
serve for dinner?"

Soon the kitchen was bubbling with wonderful smells:
roasted squash, cranberry sauce, buttery rolls,
bowls of green beans, chocolate cake, pecan pralines.

"I think we can do it!"

"We'll never eat all this!"

"They'll be here
any minute."

Rowan and Honey arrived with smiles and piles of gingersnaps and a bouquet so pretty that Berry immediately made a new leaf for the tree.

"Gingersnaps are my favorite!"

"I thought they might be."

"Thanks for inviting us!"

Once the candles were lit and their plates were full, they gave thanks for a night both bountiful and beautiful.

"Here's to the season."

After a meal most delicious, Rowan rose to propose
a toast to the hosts.

"New friends like you are the sugar
on the donut, the icing on the cake,
the cherry and whipped cream on
a chocolate milk shake."

They all laughed and agreed and added leaf after leaf to the thankful tree.

A leaf for poetry, for parties, for dancing, for singing,
and a leaf for the gift of this fabulous FRIENDSGIVING.